In the empty cottage the small boy awoke remembering two things: that this was the day of Christmas Eve and that his grandmother was not to be back for three days. Then he saw the gift his grandmother had left for him—a round red onion! Why had she left this nonsensical vegetable? What did it mean?

He abandoned the riddle and went out, but many times during that cold winter day the questions came back to haunt him. When at last the advance of night forced his return to the cottage, what was waiting? What spoke? Who answered?

Also by
Julia Cunningham

MACAROON

CANDLE TALES

DORP DEAD!

VIOLLET

Onion Journey

Onion Journey

BY JULIA CUNNINGHAM
ILLUSTRATED BY LYDIA COOLEY

PANTHEON BOOKS

For Jock *and* Larry

———————◆———————

*with love
and
love again*

Onion Journey

GILLY awoke remembering two things: that this was the day of Christmas Eve and that his grandmother was not to be with him. It would be three tomorrows before her return. He tunneled himself deeper under the quilt, as

·3

though this retreat into warmth might store enough of it within him to get through this special day without her. Then he looked out, quick-eyed, at the familiar one-room cottage: the fireplace, the table in the center, his grandmother's rocking chair, his stool, the two-shelved cupboard over the stove, the gray woolen curtains over the three small windows, made from a used-up blanket, its holes patched with blue yarn-flowers. He had been alone before. Sometimes, as now, his grandmother hired out as a housekeeper when sickness came to a family. She had trusted him to take care of himself ever since he had begun school, last year. But this day needed her. It was soon to be Christmas Eve with nothing but her magic to make it real, and she was gone.

He stayed still as long as he could and then with a sigh he slid from beneath the quilt, straightened it over the rumpled pillow, and went to the stove. He put a match to the readied kindling and placed the porridge pot over the rising heat. Then he hurried into his clothes and approached the hearth. Should he light a fire now or wait until evening? He remembered the effort it took to chop a cord of wood and turned away.

It was at this instant he saw the object

on the table. He gulped. It was a round
red onion and, beneath it, a note in
his grandmother's handwriting.

> My gift to my Gilly
> Love,
> Grandmother

For a second he thought he should laugh, but he couldn't. It wasn't a joke. They had talked together about there being no presents this year and ex-changed such understanding hugs his happiness asked for nothing more. Then why had she left this nonsensical vege-table and the note to go with it? Not to make a soup. There was food enough for her absence. For looking at? But why? It was just a common onion. He reminded himself that his grandmother was a person of many meanings. She could see the behind and beyond of things.

He spooned out a bowl of porridge,

sat on his stool, and ate; but instead of this first act of the morning marking the beginning of the adventure that each day was, the little house around him slowly seemed to expand, to stretch, to move away from him as it might from a stranger. Echoes seemed to be waiting in the corners. The flower-darns in the curtains were more like alien eyes. And, always in the middle of the room was the onion, staring at him, the gift from a grandmother who had suddenly become as much of a mystery as the shining, silken-skinned sphere in front of him.

Gilly closed his eyes. Now he could

even believe, while not believing, that the walls had receded as far as the edge of the forest beyond the meadow, pushing back the snow; that the roof had lifted itself to the height of the tallest oaks. And Gilly, himself, growing tinier and tinier.

He shivered, jerked to his feet, and, picking up the ax by the front door, went to the woodpile at the rear of the house and began to split the snow-dusted logs into sticks. After one armful he dared glance at the house. It was as it had always been, and his fear was replaced by sadness. Even the meadow was empty. No birds, no squirrels, even no night-tracks on the glassy crust of the snow. His fingers, holding the wood to his chest, numbed. Were all the forest friends tucked away in their nests and holes and burrows for Christmas? He felt himself growing foolish and tramped back into the house, depositing the wood to one side of the hearth.

Deliberately he returned to sit in the center of his grandmother's rocker, moving it very slightly back and forth with the tips of his toes, and gazed at the onion. What was its secret? He stilled the rocker, went to the cupboard, and extracted a knife. Seizing the onion with his left hand he cut deep into it a

wound six layers down. The outer peel-
ing fell off with the chunk. It sat there,
white now and shining, almost no
smaller, in the middle of grayness. The
fumes spiraled into his nose and eyes,
and moisture like tears spilled onto his
cheeks. He stood back.

Why was he bothering with this
stupid riddle? He tried to wipe the

stinging from his eyelids. He couldn't.

Something caught at Gilly. He quietly put down the knife. It was almost as though his grandmother were there, speaking to him. But before he could gather the words an assault of wind attacked the corners of the house and the presence vanished.

He shuddered with cold but did not lay a fire. He must save it for evening. He would depart from this puzzlement and go into the world to get free of it. He cut two thick slices of bread from the fat loaf in the larder, thrust the chopped-out onion pieces between them, tucked the sandwich under his jacket, wrapped his grandmother's long red scarf three times around his neck, and left the house.

Halfway across the meadow, now a monotony of snow, Gilly began to whistle. He had to interrupt the silence. It was as if every creature had been erased from this sketch of bare trees and charcoal sky. Between the seventh note and the eighth he stopped. A very little sound had intruded on his song. He listened, rooted in the snow. Again it came—the tail end of a chirp. He stepped to his left and looked down. There, in a hole as small as itself, lay a tumbled bird, its lids almost shut, its twiglike legs stuck out sideways from under its spread, quivering wings.

Gently, gently, Gilly cupped his hand around the fragile body and lifted it to his face. He held the bird to his

right ear. From what seemed as faraway as his grandmother came the tap, tap, tap of the tiny heartbeat. With his left hand he stowed the onion sandwich deeper into his coat and then tucked the bird just under his own heart, above a button where it could not slip down.

Then, walking more cautiously, for now he had someone to take care of, he continued to the border of the meadow and into the first line of oaks. The wind had dropped, but Gilly wished it would take up its snort and howl because the new soundlessness, walled in by the massive, black tree trunks, was beginning to fill with a kind of threat, as though a crowd of mute monsters might be concealed just behind the next stand of trees.

He tried to shrug off this childishness. What was the matter with him anyway? These woods were his, inch by

inch, in summer or in winter. For years
the friendship of the sun and grass and
rain, the flowers, saplings, animals had
kept him joyful. What made of all these
things, remembered and around him, an
enemy today?

He was now entering the pine grove and the pale light lessened, becoming a kind of false dusk. The smell of the heavily needled branches swirled about his face and, mingled with it as he moved, a breath of onion. Could this be what was infecting his thoughts? He found a clump of giant roots with just room enough for him to sit steadily among them and, wedged tight, he dipped his hand into his coat and drew out first the bird and then the sandwich. But before he could put the sandwich on his lap the bird let out one strong cheep and took to the air. Gilly sud-

denly wished for wings so that he might follow his one companion for at least as long as it would take the sharp jab of loneliness to evaporate. But the bird had gone.

He bit a large hunk from the sandwich and it somehow tasted of feathers. Maybe he should go back and simply destroy the onion—cast it into boiling water, stamp it into the snow, or just throw it at the sky and not watch its fall. Then being alone would be no more than aloneness without this question to gnaw holes in each hour.

He had opened his mouth to eat again when something stirred between his

legs. He tensed into utter stillness. A brown snout poked up from a cover of needles. It was a badger. It sniffed the air, then vanished. Gilly placed the sandwich in front of the hole and waited. Three minutes, five, and then the pointed head eased out once more. It seized the sandwich, drew it in after itself, and Gilly was curiously satisfied. The bird, the badger, and now his

lunch, were gone. The nearness of the snow-covered ground crept up his legs and through his body.

He gripped a root and pulled himself to his feet. He looked for a drier shelter and found it above him. Awkward with chill, he climbed slowly into the giant pine whose branches formed an irregular ladder. Choosing a wide notch between trunk and branch, he stretched his legs lengthwise and propped his back against the trunk. The slight sway of the tree was like the motion of his grandmother's rocker, and before he realized it had come, sleep closed his eyes and his mind.

When he awoke the stale taste in his mouth brought back the brief nightmare of a moment ago. He had been in the center of a vast field of onions that must be dug up before sunrise and all he had to do it with was a crooked stick and one hour of time. The shards of the dream began to reassemble, as though to encase him in a sightless, airless cask. He skinned down the tree and hurriedly walked anywhere.

The darkness was a truer darkness now, with evening just over the nearest hill. He knew he should head for home and a warming fire, but the vision of the onion, waiting lopsided on the table, barred his direction and he strode farther into the pines.

Suddenly he stumbled. He looked at his feet. There was the round hoop of a trap and caught inside it a tall brown hare. The animal's eyes were wide with panic but its movements against the steel that had captured its forepaws were feeble. Gilly broke off a two-foot branch from the nearest tree, rummaged beneath the snow until his hand grasped a stone the size of the hare's head, then inserted the branch into the teeth of the trap and bore down on it as hard as he could. The jaws opened and he quickly placed the stone between them. As gently as his touch on the bird he lifted the hare out onto the snow. The fore-paws were not broken, for with a single wild and backward stare the animal humped itself free of Gilly's hand and leaped into vanishment.

Gilly wished a second wish, as foolish

as the first, that he might be magically shrunk and able to ride the hare's back into its burrow.

He was hungry now and his weight seemed to have doubled, his feet great clods attached to his aching legs. But there was no welcome in the thought of the lonely house in the meadow where no voice but his own could answer him.

The wind was running again, erratic-
ally, in little cuts and slashes, and a thin
kind of moaning had started up before
him. He picked up the pine branch and
tried not to imagine it a weapon.

Then he saw them, glowing at him
from the core of a bush—two emerald
eyes. The dusk was so intense that
nothing showed around them. He
headed for home. He tried not to run.
He tried to tell himself that this was his
forest, a place that had protected and
delighted him for all the years of his
life, that such a friend does not crazily
become treacherous and evil. But his
thoughts melted like the vagrant fall of

snowflakes on his cheeks, leaving no trace but terror.

Something seemed to crackle at his heels. He broke into a lope. Was he imagining a pattering and a padding behind him? He reached the meadow's edge and forced his head to turn. The eyes were still there, but now they seemed to belong to a standing creature, still with no form or outline. He wanted to face this thing, whatever it was, but there was not enough strength in him. Instead he raced for the house, tore open the door, and slammed it after him. He flicked the latch down, grabbed up an armful of kindling and two logs, and shoved them into the fireplace. The pine branch had fallen under the table. He lighted a match to the spindling sticks and in the next moment the flames were rising up and into the chimney.

He squatted before the fire, hunched as close together as he could, and imagined his grandmother. He roughly drew her short roundness in his mind, her face that to no one but Gilly was beautiful, her surprisingly long-fingered hands that could take away pain and give comfort. But just as the image began to become real within him he heard a sound at the door, as though someone or something had leaned upon it.

In two motions he picked up the onion in one hand and the pine branch in the other and went toward the menace. But before he raised the latch he looked at himself, armed with onion and branch, and remembered his own cold and hunger and fear. He dropped them both and slowly opened the door wide.

Nothing. No one. He paused for a moment, but all that spoke or moved was the icy seepage of air from the outer night. He refastened the latch and looked into the room.

It had changed. The colors were restored to it: the yarn-flowers blue as flax, the rocker golden in the light of

the fire, and the whitewashed walls as fresh as an acre of daisies. A slow smile curved his mouth. And as he put his oatmeal on the stove and lighted the interior, he thought he saw the rocker stir. Maybe the entry of the wind had caused it. He cut himself a piece of bread and from the cupboard he took out a jar of his grandmother's strawberry preserves, remembering the summer day he had picked the berries. He measured two exact spoonfuls onto a plate. His feast was prepared. But there was something else to be done.

He picked up the pine branch and fitted it into an earthenware jug, unwound the red scarf from his neck and wrapped it around the base of the jug, and then centered it on the table. He sat down on his stool into quietness, and the hours reversed. They seemed to turn as on a wheel. The bird, instead of leaving him lonely, sang for him. The badger, instead of depriving him of his food, shared it with him. The hare, instead of reflecting his own fear, was grateful. And the emerald eyes, twice glimpsed, changed into a deep blue and looked at him with a sweetness that matched his grandmother's.

And, last, he looked at the onion and all the disappointment and anger and misunderstanding was gone. He saw the true shape of it. It was like love, layer upon layer of unending mystery, but to be tasted and smelled and seen in all of its loveliness. His grandmother had wanted him to know this and now he knew.

A smile he did not even realize illumined his face. He took the onion, and by means of the hole he had once dug into it, set it onto the top of the branch that was now a tree in the red-wrapped jug. And before he settled himself into the joy of the food and the fire and the empty rocker that was now not empty at all, he saw that to him the onion was not an onion but a star.

About the Author and Illustrator

———◆●◆———

JULIA CUNNINGHAM, a writer with a unique gift for poetic expression, has won wide recognition as the author of *Dorp Dead!*, *Viollet*, *Candle Tales*, and *Macaroon*.

Born in Spokane, Washington, Miss Cunningham attended a variety of schools from New York to Virginia, but considers herself self-educated.

Miss Cunningham lived for some time in France, and now is settled in Santa Barbara, California, where she is a bookseller when she is not writing.

LYDIA COOLEY studied at the University of California at Los Angeles and the Art Students' League. She has taught fine arts at California's Ojai Valley School and her paintings have been exhibited at the Whitney Museum of American Art and the Santa Barbara Museum of Art. Miss Cooley also makes her home in Santa Barbara.